UNIT 12

Jeremy Jae Jae Davis

See It Through

Merie Vision Publishing
Merievisionpublishing@gmail.com

Copyright © 2024 by Jeremy "Jac-Jac" Davis
Uptown Classic Productions

ISBN: 978-1-961213-12-8

Library of Congress control number on record

Formatting, Editing, and Design by
Merie Vision Publishing, LLC

First Print Edition: October 2024

Printed in the United States of America

Chapter 1
LAPD

Antwan grew up admiring his father, Detective Dwayne Jacobs, a decorated Los Angeles police detective with 22 years of service. As part of a special task force, Detective Jacobs and his team investigated high-level corruption, including bribery, extortion, embezzlement, police brutality, and misuse of power amongst police and government officials in the states of California, Montana, and Nevada.

This exposure had a profound impact on Antwan's upbringing and shaped his desire to combat injustice alongside his father. He wanted to serve as a role model and bridge the gap between law enforcement and his community by providing a much-needed perspective that valued de-escalation measures over their "shoot-first" tactics. Because of this, it didn't take much for him to know exactly what he wanted to do with his life.

After he graduated from high school, he and his father decided to go to their favorite vacation getaway in Montana's famous Yellow Stone National Park before life changed for the both of them. This trip was special because it was not only their normal father-son retreat. This trip signified something greater. Detective Jacobs had bought a beautiful estate in the area so that he and his son could get away from reality and reset from all the woes of life. Normally, the estate would be rented out to others for various vacations, but they made sure to take advantage of the times the estate was not rented out. Usually, the summertime was always the time they both looked forward to and expected.

During this time, the warm sunlight filtered through the window, casting a comforting glow on the plush furnishings that invited you to sink in and unwind. The scent of freshly brewed coffee wafted from the kitchen and mingled with the subtle aroma of pine and earth. Just a few hundred feet away from the estate, you could hear the roaring sounds of the nearby Yellow Stone River, as it lulled you into a state of tranquility. The entire aura transported you to a place where time literally stood still.

Dwayne had been bringing Antwan up to the rocky mountain wilderness of Montana since he was a toddler. It was said that few people called it home, making it truly one of the most peaceful places to live. Nobody the Jacobs' knew resided in Montana and nobody in Montana seemed to know anyone who lived outside of Montana.

It just seemed like the perfect place to retreat and find solace after the long stressful months of being a LAPD detective. Buying property in the mountains, chopping your own firewood, growing your own vegetables, and living off the grid had always been the plan for Dwayne the day he retired.

Throughout the years, he would often take this time to teach his son primitive skills as well. Antwan grew up shooting various guns. By the time he'd turned seven, he could shoot and hit a moving target from 150 yards in the distance with a gun or bow and arrow. He could also climb a tree in twenty seconds flat. Amazingly, he could hold his breath underwater for two full minutes while spearfishing. His father also taught him several camouflage techniques to make it harder to be seen, and easier to hunt. His survival skills would continue to improve as he grew older.

Outside of the estate, the towering trees swayed softly in the breeze and created a sense of seclusion and peace as if the world had slowed down just for them. This was Dwayne's getaway... *his peace of mind*...the staycation refuge he'd longed to live out for the remainder of his life. He could not wait to retire and stay on the estate long-term. Yet, both, Antwan and Detective Jacobs, didn't know just how drastically their life was about to change

Two months later...

After returning home to Los Angeles, following in the footsteps of his beloved father, Antwan enrolled in the police academy. Jacobs was a laid-back and chill officer. He didn't give off the normal asshole cop kind of vibe as the majority of the LA cops did. Whenever he drove into the drug and gang-infested

3

neighborhoods, the residents were always happy to see him. The gangbangers and drug dealers didn't like him, but in all, they respected him. It wasn't because he was a black officer, it was more so the fact that he overlooked what his white counterparts didn't.

Antwan eventually passed the California Highway Patrol (CHP) written exam with flying colors. He also aced the six-month course and received his service certification two months prior to his scheduled graduation. He went in fully prepared for the exam, due to his father picking his brain daily to prep him for the exam.

Not only did his test results catch the eyes of his recruiting officers, but word had spread quickly around LAPD headquarters about a top prospect who graduated with honors and was said to be reporting to the third precinct.

Jacobs was ecstatic about his retirement because this meant he would be back to living life peacefully on his estate in Montana. His initial goal before retirement was to be Antwan's ride-along partner for a couple of weeks. That way he could help his son get the authentic experience of being a cop while learning from his father's guidance and professional perspective.

Now, it was time to hang up his Tom Ford, double-breasted suit, and back into a blue uniform. Detective Jacobs had just enough time to teach Antwan the do's and don'ts of policing, but he had no plans on staying any longer than his expected retirement date.

Just thirty days, six hours, and fourteen minutes, he mumbled to himself while looking down at his expensive one-of-one Audemar Piguet royal oak watch.

Los Angeles Police Department 3rd precinct...

Antwan was overwhelmed with excitement. He entered the precinct and walked directly toward the commander's desk.

"Good evening! I'm Antwan Jacobs, reporting for duty."

The older blonde-haired woman pulled her glasses up from her nose, looking him directly in his eyes. "Jacobs! You were supposed to be assigned to partner with Officer V. Gomez, but my paperwork states Detective Jacobs, who is also your father, will be joining you instead. Let's get this understood now, for future reference, there will be no special privileges here. I don't care who your father is, we are all equal under the shield. You are here to do one thing and one thing only – to serve and protect. I'm pretty sure your father has told you this already."

"Yes ma'am, he has. May I ask your name?" he asked.

"I'm your shift commander, Alice Lorain Smith," she replied, looking surprised as if he was supposed to know her name. "I'm the person you will be reporting to every morning at muster for your assignments, districts, and routes, which are always subjected to change. I will see you at zero five hundred

5

hours, no excuses." She said while closing her login book. "These are the keys to your police cruiser, number twenty-one. You lucked up Jacobs. That's one of our newer vehicles," she said, passing him the keys.

"Thank you," he replied before returning to the chaotic precinct.

The energy was thick. It felt like being the new kid in a new city that's transferring to a new school. He could feel that all eyes were definitely on him. Several officers approached and introduced themselves along with their ranks. Some were stern, others were down to earth. One captain couldn't help himself, he told racist jokes and talked about how Donald Trump would make our economy and America *great* again. Antwan Just smiled, agreed, and kept it moving. His father taught him, in every joke told there is always some form of truth behind it. So, while he laughed, he was also taking mental notes. *I can't believe I'm actually a LAPD police officer,* he said to himself for the hundredth time as he entered his father's office.

"There goes my boy!!" Dwayne yelled excitedly as he stood up hugging his son. "You're looking sharp in that uniform, son. Reminds me of myself over twenty-five years ago not having a clue what this journey was going to become or what I would get out of it. But son, I couldn't be prouder of you," he said as the two embraced. Dwayne recollected back to when he first arrived at the third precinct. *Twenty years ago* – he'd done so much in that small window of time.

Some decisions he regretted making. If he could take them back he would, but it came a time in his career when he just wanted to be able to look back and honestly ask himself was the journey really worth it? Unfortunately, a big dilemma held his retirement date at bay. Just recently, Dwayne received word from his best friend, Anthony Hayes, who was down at the federal internal affairs office in Norfolk, Virginia.

He stated to Dwayne that he was allegedly under a federal investigation indictment for bribery extortion, embezzlement, tampering with evidence, false arrest, excessive use of force, civil rights violations, and conspiracy to defraud the government. He was then informed that his indictment could lead to criminal penalties, fines, and potentially a severe lengthy prison sentence. It was at that very moment he knew he had to come up with a master plan.

After diligently putting in hundreds of hours of planning and brainstorming, what he finally came up with was sure to shake up the entire police force, the state of California, Nevada, and the federal authorities across the United States. Dwayne snapped out of his daydream. He looked over at his son seconds before entering their vehicle and said, "Just know the world that you knew yesterday will no longer exist after today. As first responders, we get an intimate, first-hand glimpse of the evil that's in our world. Mentally, this job can be challenging, but know your purpose, and stand on your beliefs. I promise you there will be no obstacle that can get in your way."

As soon as they entered the squad car, Dwayne looked over and said, "Son, I know the love and passion you have in your heart, but this job doesn't pay us enough to be superheroes. It is a fact that we're here to protect and serve our community and the people living in it, but use your common sense. Always assess the situation before moving forward, and that's when you make a calculated decision. Remember, always, no matter what, call for backup. Even if you feel as though you can handle it, the most chaotic situations always start off calm, cool, and collected. So, it's always good to know that someone has your back. The same goes for you. No matter how small it may seem, always and I mean always, back your partner. Keep in mind, this job gives you the power to be able to save a life or take one. Your backup will most likely give you the security you may need in order to execute your decision. Follow these steps, and you will successfully climb your way up the policing ladder of success."

Chapter 2
The Mole

Their operations were always confidential stings. For all they knew, their police headquarters had no clue of the number of times they raided secret dope stashes and stopped immigrants daily crossing the border loaded with drugs, guns, and cash. The twenty-four members of Unit 12 had been investigating this particular cartel for months, and through intel, they knew their every move. Dwayne and his unit were just about to call it quits when their targeted U-Haul truck was spotted on their radar around midnight.

Instead of the usual petite, Spanish woman who normally drove, the U-Haul was occupied by three male occupants this time. Their confidential informant revealed to them that the load contained bales of cocaine and United States currency.

Human trafficking had become one of the largest profits for the cartel since Covid. That explained the sudden rise in Amber alerts for missing and exploited women and children lately. You just never know or could prepare yourself for what's in those vehicles crossing over the border.

With everyone in their assigned places, it was now time to move in. As head of the unit, Jacobs led the pack, dressed in his tactical black bulletproof gear, while holding his M-16 assault rifle with the night vision scope. He began creeping up alongside the vehicle.

The immigrants never saw it coming. In one instance, they were ambushed and detained. Two guns and a bulletproof vest were found under the passenger seat. Jacobs and other officers began to gather their information, when he suddenly heard, "Bingo!"

Officer Jones yelled as bails of money began falling out of the back of the U-Haul truck. They stood there looking in awe. Officer Jones was Jacobs' partner and he couldn't have been more excited.

"This has to be millions in cold hard cash. We can all use a nice vacation with this lick."

Jacobs walked over and began unwrapping one of the brown papers that held the currency, which revealed a wad of money. He held it in his hands and flipped through each bill making sure it wasn't counterfeit. That's when he looked down again and noticed the thirty-thousand-dollar bank band around it. Twenty years on the force taught him two things about the cartel, and one was that they don't mind if a load gets busted that's paying their taxes. They hate for their money to get intercepted, confiscated, or stolen.

"Let's get this truck to our secured location for now. Before we leave, Officer Williams, can you check the U-Haul for any tracking devices? It's no way the cartel loaded this truck with this much currency without a way of tracking it down."

"What do we do with the Mexicans? If we let them go, it's going to look like a robbery and the cartel won't take light of this." Officer Jones stated with concern.

" My suggestion is that we take them to the middle of the Mojave and kill them all!" Officer Jones added. "Well, look at the fleas on fluffy!" Officer Williams said walking up and holding the tracking device he just discovered in his right hand. "It was located under the dashboard," he said, interrupting their conversation, "Looks like we're good to go."

Detective Jacobs shook his head and addressed what was being said before he was rudely interrupted. "Killing them won't be necessary, just let them go! They're already going to have to worry about the cartel killing them! Let that blood be on their hands. This way, I feel better about us keeping the money." Detective Jacobs replied.

Officer Williams and Jones felt like the best thing to do was kill them. That way, there would be no clues left as to who, what, when, or why. That was something Unit 12 prided their tactics on, but tonight Detective Jacobs wasn't following their protocol. What could they do? He called the shots, and like always, they followed his direction. Officer Jones uncuffed the three immigrants and shot his pistol twice into the air yelling for them to run off! The other officers looked on in disgust as the men ran as fast as they could through the cold dark desert and headed towards the mountains.

Then, Officer Jones handed Detective Jacobs a note that was discovered in the glove compartment, which confirmed the total amount of the money found to be a hundred million.

"Damn! Split that twelve ways and that's eight hundred and thirty-three thousand apiece," Jones said rubbing his hands together.

Everyone agreed and they all headed back to headquarters to split the lick.

This was just one of many robberies they stole from the cartel. Each Captain of Unit 12 was a multi-millionaire, but they all lived in million-dollar mansions, owned private jets, and drove foreign cars. Unit 12 members were certified rock stars. Every cop in the third precinct wanted to become a part of this special task force, but the only way in was by sacrifice and the only way out was death, illness, or retirement.

Officer Jones, Smith, Parker, Williams, Davis, Kelly, Moore, Skyler, Perkins, Brown, Jacobs, and their infamous leader, Brock Ranson, were all a part of Unit 12, a twelve man SWAT tactical unit. Their new assignment was to protect the border from illegal drug immigrants crossing over. This had to be one of their luckiest nights ever.

As the team searched the area, they came upon two immigrants. One had a bottle of water and the other had two oranges, a map of the Mojave desert, and two shovels tied to their backs. From the looks of it, they looked exhausted, thirsty, and dirty. Perkins knew from experience they had just buried the drugs and were returning in the early hours to retrieve them. Years of training and hundreds of arrests had taught him what red flags to look for.

After detaining the two immigrants, they began searching the area and came upon five six-foot stash holes in the ground. From their observation, it looked to be full of bales of cocaine. Jacobs had yet to report it to border patrol or customs as he usually would have. By the looks on the faces of his unit, he could tell that they didn't want him to either.

"What the hell are we supposed to do with all these drugs?" he asked while holding his hands on top of his head in a frustrating manner.

"We can sell them!" Both officers said in unison.

"So, now we're drug dealers too?" Jacobs asked. "We took an oath and swore to uphold the law."

"Man, we tarnished that oath the minute we began robbing the cartel!" Officer Williams shouted. "We have clients already prepared to handle shipments like these. It's almost a cash and carry. As soon as the buyer realize all the drugs are legit, he won't hesitate to cut the check. I've seen shipments like these go for forty-million on the black market. That's a quick three hundred thousand for each of us. I'd say that's a clean getaway! Nobody ever knows but us, and them dead amigos."

Jacobs was adamant about not allowing his officers to kill the two immigrants. For all he knew, they were being used as mules to get the drugs across the border. He personally uncuffed them and sent them running through the desert as well.

"That's going to come back and seriously hurt us!" Officer Jones said shaking his head.

"We're not killing for this shit!" Jacobs said in a stern tone.

"Then you're on the wrong team and playing the wrong game. No matter how you look at it, this type of money comes with blood on it, and killing is the only way we're going to be able to keep it. It's just a matter of time, and the cartel is going to want to know who keeps robbing them. I don't think Chief Lewis would like hearing about us allowing drug mules to roam free back into the desert to tell on us."

"Chief Lewis can kiss my black ass! This is my unit and whoever don't like the way I operate can freely leave you will be replaced." Jacobs said in a cocky tone.

He already knew most of the officers in Unit 12 didn't care too much for him and his patriotic blue-blood characteristics. For them, upholding the law wasn't a part of the plan.

14

Hitting the streets....

Breaking out of his daydream, Jacobs realized how far they had driven into the city. Antwan was amazed how drivers seemed to tense up as they drove up beside them. "Now I see how cops recognize when someone is nervous, pops."

Antwan looked to his left and observed a four-door midnight blue Lexus LS 460. It was occupied by four male teenagers. All of them were sitting up straight, seatbelts on, and driving the speed limit. No music could be heard from outside of their vehicle either.

"How odd is that?" Dwayne asked looking over at Antwan. It had a red flag written all over it. "That's a sign you can always look for, son. The nervousness of the driver is always a giveaway. Now, all you have to do is follow them, and wait until they make a traffic violation."

Antwan looked over at the vehicle and said, "They're not bothering anyone. I'm going to let them live today," he said looking back in his father's direction.

"That's your choice, son," he replied.

For the next five minutes, they cruised down Crenshaw Blvd until they heard a call over the radio for a 211 in progress at 3150 Wilshire Blvd.

"That's a robbery, correct?" Antwan asked.

15

"You got it!" Jacobs replied as Antwan hit his siren and the gas pedal at the same time heading towards the crime scene. "It's never a dull day serving and protecting in LA. I can assure you."

Within minutes, they arrived at the Wells Fargo Federal Bank. Several FBI and CIA agents blocked off the intersection and began casing the area. Detective Jacobs was still recognized and highly respected even in his blue uniform. Officers securing the area allowed him access inside of the bank.

Once inside, he received a debriefing from Lieutenant King, a twenty-five-year veteran on the force. He was the acting officer in charge of the investigation. He was standing alongside the bank manager, Mrs. Greene, when they entered the bank. In her statement, she reported that it was four armed assailants all wearing masks. From the bank's video surveillance, they drove away in a blue four-door Lexus LS 460, headed North on Wilshire Blvd.

The man behind the plan....

Unit 12 had been under investigation for the past three years. Their commander-in-chief, Ranson, was a real dickhead! He was a crooked cop who had just been demoted to administration leave while under investigation until further notice, but he was still allowed to work. Unbeknownst to him, Detective Jacobs was just assigned as the mole in his unit. His assigned mission was to investigate, collect evidence, and expose the corruption within Unit 12 without blowing his cover.

Officer Williams called Detective Jacobs to tell him he'd just recently scheduled the meetup with the black-market client. Detective Jacobs wasn't giving anyone the "go to sell," unless he was present himself.

The ride seemed forever, but after two hours of back roads, they finally arrived. The location was in the Hollywood Hills, home to some of the wealthiest people in California. Jacobs knew whoever was purchasing these drugs were definitely the real deal the minute they arrived. This estate had to be one of the biggest and most exquisite works of craftsmanship he'd ever seen done.

The front entrance was grand. Upon arriving, they were stopped at the security gate where two guards searched them and their vehicle for weapons. They proceeded to drive up to the estate where several men stood awaiting. Two of the men looked familiar and the closer they approached the more recognizable the individuals became to Detective Jacobs. It was, without a doubt, the man known around the precinct as Captain Perkins and Peter Carter, standing alongside several other unknown affiliates.

Dwayne knew this was the intel he needed to crack this investigation.

"Detective Jacobs!" Perkins said in his most welcoming tone. "I see you've decided to take a trip to the other side. The department's retirement pension isn't as welcoming as this estate, huh? You will never experience a portion of this lifestyle with their 401k," he said laughing.

"Walk with me," Peter Carter said as he and Dwayne separated themselves from the others and began walking the beautiful landscape. Detective Jacobs noticed, to his far left, just around three hundred yards away, sat the famous Hollywood sign overlooking the city of Los Angeles, California. "You know we bust our asses and risk our lives every day to get paid less than a hundred grand a year. I'm in a position now where I spend that shit in a day, and don't think twice about it. I just want my piece of the multibillion-dollar American pie too! I've confiscated hundreds of millions in money and drugs for the government. It's been times when I couldn't afford to pay my mortgage or even take my wife on a nice vacation. Make it make sense- I believe we both deserve to live this lifestyle, don't you agree?"

"Hell yeah!" Jacobs agreed. "So, this is the reason internal affairs have you under investigation?"

"Part of it," Peter Carter replied. "Allegedly, I was stealing bricks of coke and heroin from cartel seizures out of the evidence lockers and replacing them with synthetic ones."

"That was creative," Jacobs replied.

"Not enough! Somehow, someone caught on and reported it to internal affairs. I think it was someone in Unit 12. That's how this all began," he said spreading his arms.

"So, you stole the drugs?" Jacobs asked.

"Hell yeah! It's enough money out here for us all to live the remainder of our lives like royalty. The police and government have always been corrupt Jacobs. Mexico cartels will forever be allowed to operate and flood the United States as long as they can tax."

"How is the government taxing the cartel? Jacobs asked.

"Through ICE. We catch the immigrants, detain them, and charge the Mexican government for housing them. In return, they get fully compensated by the cartel. It's a big money game being played right in our faces. Why do you think Trump didn't complete building the wall? That would have shut down a hundred billion dollar a year business. It's no such thing as a war on drugs. I can promise you, it won't stop with us! So, why not enjoy the fruits of our labor? Why – we have the sweetest opportunity. You agree?"

"Absolutely," Jacobs replied.

"Now, let's get down to business. We have a client waiting," Carter said walking away.

Dwayne began following behind him, on his personal quest for more information, but moving cautiously knowing that he was bugged.

Chapter 3
Getting Beat On The Beat

"Lesson number one, we survive off of instinct. In our profession, we follow our gut feeling. We both can agree that those kids in the Lexus looked suspicious right?"

"Yes sir!" Antwan replied.

"So, next time, I will follow my gut feeling no matter what," Antwan replied, pulling back into the station, and ending his shift.

Detective Jacobs was finally locked in with one of the dirtiest cops in LA. Today, he was to meet back up with Peter Carter to receive 10 million in cash, and the other ten would be wired to his offshore account in Belize. Detective Jacobs arrived at the Carter estate, anticipating bullshit to occur, but in actuality, Carter had cash money and the wired account numbers ready to send to Jacobs' destination. He also explained to him that he answered to someone by the name of Brock Ranson, the commander and chief of their entire operation. "He calls the shots and what he says is law."

"Is he here?" Jacobs asked.

"No," Peter Carter replied. "His location and whereabouts are top secret classified information. We only communicate with Ranson through Captain Perkins and our radios. We take care of our own," he said shaking Detective Jacobs' hand. "This gentleman here, is Alex Applegate, our personal realtor. I'm pretty sure he can help you find a beautiful estate here in the hills."

"That wasn't in my plans, until I figured out how I was going to get around the IRS," Detective Jacobs replied.

"Oh, no worries. We have that covered, too. Right now, it's all about allowing you to live the real American dream," Peter Carter said as he walked away.

I didn't sign up for this...

The beat became everything his Father told him it would be – literally a hot mess! A regular day would consist of several domestic violence altercations, about five public intoxications, a few petty drug and prostitution busts, and a couple of speeding tickets. Then, Antwan would call it a night. Unfortunately, after two weeks on the ride along, his father decided to part ways with him

Dwayne explained to his son that he had a very important assignment that he was sent to do and he would eventually reveal it to him at the appropriate time. The following Monday morning, Antwan's new partner was standing alongside his squad car, awaiting his arrival.

Patrol Officer Gomez was a five-foot even, 145-pound, curvaceous bombshell. At first glance, she reminded him of the Latin sensation Shakira.

"Hello! I'm officer Gomez. You must be my partner, Antwan Jacobs?" she asked while holding her small hand out."

"Pleased to meet you," he replied totally caught off guard by her beautiful appearance.

She also noticed and said, "Don't let this small package fool you. I'm a tough little cookie," she said, winking her eye while entering the passenger side of the squad vehicle.

"So, what made you want to become a cop instead of a model Gomez?" He asked in awe of her beauty.

"Aww, thank you," she replied. "I come from a bloodline of drug dealers and killers. I've witnessed firsthand the devastation it brings to families and their communities. Knowing my family lineage, I wanted to be the one who made a difference and change the narrative of the Gomez family name."

Just minutes into their conversation, they received their first call from dispatch – a 10-40 assault and battery was in progress.

Antwan hit dispatch back. "Unit #77, Officer Jacobs and Gomez en route."

"Ten four!" the voice over the radio responded.

"Okay, Gomez, our first call!" he said, turning on his siren while speeding and weaving through the busy downtown Los Angeles intersection.

Ranson executed so many weekly drug busts that they had to set up a restricted warehouse to store the stolen money and cocaine. Even though they had clientele on the black market and sold vast shipments, they would always have extra bales of cocaine and illegal weapons just sitting around. Dwayne began stealing two kilos per bale, replacing them with synthetic ones, which added up to a total of ten kilos per week. He was determined to take down Ranson and the entire Unit 12.

Once a month, Detective Jacobs would take a private jet to his luxurious estate. It was there where he stored the evidence in his underground bunker and the evidence he had on Ranson was beginning to pile up. Not only did he have audio voice recordings of their conversations, he also had ample video footage of the stolen weapons and drugs, seized from the illegal immigrants crossing the border. It was only a matter of time before he would single-handedly take down one of the biggest police corruption operations since the Reagan administration.

Detective Jacobs knew he had Ranson and his team of pawns in the chokehold. Now, all he had to do was call Bo Rodgers down at the United States Federal District Attorney's office. The two were partners for more than ten years. Bo retired from law enforcement and became one of the top District Attorney's in

California, but Detective Jacobs knew for decades that Rodgers was dirty. He was still eating from the table of corruption. His chair just switched and now he's doing his dirt in the United States Federal Courts.

A waste of tax dollars......

The neighborhood was engulfed with police officers when they arrived. Antwan had to park almost two hundred feet away from the residents. Crowds of people were yelling and screaming at the top of their lungs. The officers already on the scene just couldn't seem to get the chaos in order. After listening for a couple of minutes, Jacobs decided to step in. He knew from training to separate the two parties.

He kindly asked two women to walk over so he could speak with them near his squad car, while his partner Gomez debriefed the gentleman. After interviewing both parties, the officers met back up and came to a conclusion based on both parties' statements.

Allegedly the husband came home drunk and began his verbal domestic tirade on his wife. No one was physically assaulted. Jacobs concluded that it was just a big, loud argument causing an unnecessary scene and a loss of taxpayer dollars. I have to make it to detective status as soon as possible. *Working the beat is not the kind of police work I imagined myself doing*, he said to himself in a frustrating tone while getting back into his squad car and driving away.

Federal District Attorney's office...

"Well, shut the front door!" Bo Rodgers yelled excited by the information Detective Jacobs had just relayed to him. "So, where is the evidence stored?"

"I can't tell you over the phone, but whenever we meet up, I'll give you the full details. I've put in too much work for this operation to fail."

"Understood, do you need me to meet you somewhere?" Bo asked.

"No. I'm just giving you a heads up, so I won't get indicted along with Ranson and his entire Unit 12."

"Well, that's noted in my federal investigation file," Bo replied. "Good job by the way. Remember, the sooner you get me that evidence, the quicker I can process the warrants and get the judge to sign the indictments."

"That's a ten four," Detective Jacobs replied.

"It's officers like you that's making America great again!" Bo yelled into the phone.

"Thanks, Bo. I joined the force to serve and protect foreign and domestic. Certain lines just can't be crossed. I'll call you next week," Detective Jacobs said before unhooking his recorder box and hanging up.

He never held a conversation without recording it. He knew how important this operation was and he'd be damned if he was going to allow it to slip through his fingers.

With Antwan scoring one of the highest test scores of his class, it helped his plea for a promotion. Two months and seventeen days later he was called into the office for a meeting with Deputy Chief Warren Lewis, a hard nose, no nonsense type of guy. The minute Antwan entered his office, a profuse amount of cigar smoke entered his lungs and he began coughing immediately.

"Aww, sit your virgin lung having ass down!" the Chief said with a scratchy voice, "You youngsters got good lungs. Here, try this," he said, passing Antwan his lit cigar.

Antwan was a nonsmoker,but he didn't want to seem rude, so he puffed it lightly and passed it back. Chief Lewis laughed at the disgruntled expression on Antwan's face, while opening his police record.

"Looking at your file, I see you just recently graduated from the academy top of the class, huh?"

"Yes, I did sir!" Antwan replied while sitting up straight.

"That's amazing," Chief Lewis replied. "But that don't mean shit! Paperwork and experience are two different things. I have a position available in one of my best units. There, you can get the experience along with the credentials you'll need. I see you rising through the ranks fairly easily."

"Well, I'm definitely looking forward to it Chief."

"Officer Kendall Bryant was one of my best officers. Unfortunately, he was shot and killed in the line of duty while out on a secret operation. I'm going to need to replace him immediately. You think you're up for the job?"

"Yes sir!" Antwan confidently answered.

"You will be teaming up with the tactical team within the next seventy-two hours. Your job is to oversee and back up their operations."

"So basically, I'm the reinforced help when needed?" Antwan asked.

"For the moment. Everyone starts off in training. These are your assignment papers. You are to report to special agent Perkins. Thank you for your service. I'm looking forward to hearing great things about you."

Antwan stood up and thanked him for the opportunity before exiting his office. He exited out of the Deputy Chief's office and there she was. Gomez was there standing with her hands on her hips cheering him on smiling, clapping, and jumping up and down as if he'd just received his high school diploma. Even though their partnership was cut short, their connection wasn't. Officer Gomez made Antwan pinky promise her that taco Tuesdays and wild out Wednesdays at Roscoe's Chicken and Waffles were a lock. "Without a doubt," Antwan replied. "You can always count me in for Roscoe's Chicken and Waffles."

It was a bittersweet moment because he loved being around Gomez's pretty ass. She was an amazing person and partner, but it was no denying the physical attraction he harbored since their first ride along. He knew it wasn't conducive to their working partnership. So, he was more than happy to get the promotion.

Bo Rodgers wasn't who he was portrayed to be. After all, he'd been on Ranson's payroll for over the last two years. He called him the moment he and Detective Jacobs finished their conversation.

"Bo no good azz Rodgers! It been a whole week. I know you have something essential for me?" Ranson said, answering his phone.

"I do boss! As of now, I have recorded conversations between me and Jacobs, and the evidence he has so far seems to be damning! It looks as if he has to be dealt with accordingly. He loves the shield and bleeds blue. I can't see him conforming over to this lifestyle."

"What the hell is wrong with people nowadays – just happy being piss poor and living check to check," Ranson said, walking back and forth in his downtown luxury penthouse office.

The thing is, he couldn't kill Detective Jacobs without retrieving the stolen evidence that he admitted to stealing from the warehouse.

3rd precinct Los Angeles CA...

Dective Jacobs was transitioning out of being the Captain of Unit 12 due to his retirement coming up, so he gave out orders and assignments from his desk back at the precinct. Captain Perkins had been assigned to take over as the leader of the unit the day Detective Jacobs retired. Until then, Detective Jacobs was still the H.N.I.C.

At zero seventeen hundred hours muster call the following morning, breaking and entering of Detectives Jacobs' home was to be executed. Ranson assigned that mission to Officer Kelly, one of the dirtiest cops and strategic killer he'd ever known. He was also responsible for the murder of Officer Bryant. The set-up happens to be quick and efficient.

Unit 12 received an anonymous call around zero two hundred hours later stating that immigrants were near the Mojave border and would likely be illegally crossing over into the United States before sunrise.

By the time they all geared up and reached their destination, no one was present, and there hadn't been any signs of immigrants crossing over. From Officer Bryant's observation, there seemed to be no footrail, water bottles, nor were there oranges or banana peels lying on the ground. That was usually a clue that they were or could be near the perimeter.

After getting on his radio and calling in the bogus call to headquarters, they were instructed to return back to base. That is when Officer Bryant turned around only to notice a gun pointing directly at his head – he didn't have a chance. He was shot point blank range between his eyes, execution style. Kelly proceeded to bury the gun in the sand and immediately called for backup.

When asked what happened, Kelly responded that several immigrants had caught them off guard and ambushed them. His officer-down call over the radio involved every police officer in the state of California, leading them on a tenacious, unnecessary manhunt, looking for a ghost. Once again, wasting the taxpayers' money. It was reported that Officer Bryant wanted out of Unit 12 and Ranson honored his decision the best way he knew how. Now, Kelly's new assignment was to surveillance Detective Jacobs' every move with hopes of him leading her to the stolen evidence. He was to be ready to execute him at the appointed time.

Prior to his new assignment, he hid multiple cameras inside their storage facility and even placed a tracking device on Jacobs vehicle. Officer Kelly called to tell Ranson that everything was a go. Ranson hung up and walked over to sit at his desk. *It's just a matter of time Jacobs,* he said to himself, looking down at his police portfolio. Then, he took a red marker and circled the detective's photo.

Unit 12 headquarters...

Antwan drove I-40 a couple of hours north of Los Angeles to an undisclosed area. He turned left onto a back dirt road and proceeded to drive for two minutes until he arrived at a gated fence hosting several signs that read, Keep Out, No Trespassing, and Private

30

Property. There were also three heavily armed officers walking up to his vehicle.

Antwan flashed his badge and his assignment papers. Then, told them he was there to see Captain Perkins and that he was referred by Deputy Chief Lewis of the 3rd precinct. After confirming his identity, he was allowed into the confines of the compound. The first thing he noticed was a gigantic warehouse, a few detective vehicles, and several luxury vehicles, including a Royals Royce Phantom, two Maybachs, one Lamborghini, and two Mercedes G-wagons. He looked on in awe trying his best to understand exactly where he was.

The warehouse was located in the California Mojave desert. It was there where most of their tactical police training took place. Antwan walked through a gigantic steel door to enter. Once in, he noticed several men standing around watching several Spanish women dancing on top of the bar. He looked back at the address again just to make sure he was in the correct building. That's when special agent Perkins noticed and began walking over towards him.

"Welcome! I've been waiting on you for a couple of days. You arrived on our off day. This is just a little entertainment for the guys. Would you like a drink?"

"I wouldn't mind," Antwan said.

"Brown or white?"

"I prefer brown," Antwan replied.

Perkins walked over to the bar and returned with a pint of Hennessy. "We work our asses off out here and barely have time to enjoy times like this, but whenever we do, we make the best of it. Working the desert is a different experience. It takes a lot of guts to work out here. It's far more dangerous than working any beat, on top of dealing with the extreme weather conditions. It's survival rules when working the Mojave, and the first of many is rule number one: always know the desert can kill you in the daytime with its hot and humid climates, and it will freeze you to death at night with its low-freezing temperatures. There is also a mandated dress code when working," he said, looking at Antwan sporting his black wife beater.

"Secondly, communication is important. Always have your radio on you at all times even when you're off duty. You never know if or when one of your partners will need you to back them up. It's always a possibility you can get to him just in the nick of time to save his life. What makes us strong is our communication. Without that, any operation we conduct is subject to fail."

For some reason, Antwan felt as if he'd heard this same conversation before.

"Unfortunately, we just lost one of my best officers, Christopher Bryant. May his soul rest in peace. He was shot and killed by an immigrant crossing over our US border with bales of cocaine. What we do here is special operations. We take on missions and operations the regular police, customs, or

32

border control refuses. We operate mostly at night, catching drug smugglers, human trafficking, and immigrants illegally crossing our borders. Come over here and let me introduce you to the crew."

They walked towards a crowd of men drinking and talking. "This is Antwan Jacobs from the third precinct. I want each and every one of you to welcome him to our unit. Embrace him with love and support. He is one of us now. Within a matter of seconds, officer after officer walked over and shook his hand, welcoming him to the unit – all except one.

Antwan noticed him still sitting in his chair, drinking as if he had not a care in the world who he was. So, just out of curiosity, he waited until he knew he was looking over in his direction. That's when he made eye contact with him and pointed over in his direction. Immediately, he asked the first officer standing next to him, "What is his name?"

The officer looked over towards the bar and replied, "Oh, that's Kelly. "He's different. Don't mind him. That's just the way he is before he gets to know anyone," he said, patting Antwan on his back before walking away. Antwan wasn't bothered by far He just wanted Kelly to know that he was on to him as well.

Antwan couldn't believe he'd made it to Unit 12. This was the most talked about unit in the entire LAPD. It was rumored that they received the biggest annual bonuses due to the threat level and conditions they were required to work in.

Perkins walked back over and asked Antwan if everything was ok. He replied yes and asked him, what was the biggest bonus he'd received working Unit 12. Perkins smiled and said, "We get bonuses often, but let's just say my last one was around two million dollars. You're in a whole different tax bracket when you're a part of the unit," Perkins said.

That explained the expensive cars and jewelry he noticed everyone driving and wearing. If he didn't know any better, he would have thought they were the cartel.

Another day on the Job...

As usual, Jacobs walked out of his home at exactly 5:30 pm. He battled his entire life with having obsessive-compulsive disorder(OCD) – it's one of the reasons he is always punctual in his daily activities. The minute Detective Jacobs drove out of his driveway, Kelly exited his unmarked vehicle dressed in all black. He walked around the back of the residence, where he proceeded to break out the kitchen window before entering. He set his watch for three minutes tops.

After rummaging through several drawers and flipping his mattress, he concluded that it was nothing there. The entire house was immaculately clean. He could have easily spotted anything out of the ordinary if it was worth confiscating. Coming up short, out of frustration, he violently ripped down Jacobs' sixty-five-inch flat-screen television to try and possibly throw off investigators as if an intruder had broken in. Then, he exited out of the residence the same way he'd entered.

Once he got into his vehicle, he called Ranson with the news.

"Yeah?" he answered.

"That's a no-go boss!" Kelly said, shaking his head. "I tore the house to pieces and came up with nothing. By pulling up his GPS, I can get the drop on his location in a matter of minutes, and from there, I will conduct full surveillance on his every move."

"That's a ten-four officer," Ranson concurred.

Kelly drove off and headed towards Detective Jacobs' location.

After returning home and discovering that it had been broken into, Detective Jacobs began to assess the amount of damage and what was actually missing. His police instincts started to kick in. *For one, who's brave enough to break into a cop's house?* Not only had he lived there for more than twenty years, but he'd also parked his police cruiser in his driveway for just as long. Being a detective, he studied criminals; and from his experience, he knew that criminals normally cased out the houses they decided to break into. So, he knew this wasn't an ordinary burglary because nothing of value was actually taken – just a lot of unnecessary damage.

After spending an hour cleaning, he decided to take his trash out towards the curb because trash pickup was in the morning. He immediately looked to his left and noticed what looked to be an unmarked, unoccupied police vehicle parked in front of the

Smith's residence. It was just a hundred meters away, which was awkward. He felt that if he were to walk towards the vehicle, someone would be slumped down in their seat ready to ambush him. Just thinking of it made the hair on the back of his neck stand up. However, whoever it was, he didn't want them to know that he was on to them as well. So, he walked back into his residence and observed the suspicious vehicle throughout the remainder of the night from his bedroom window.

Detective Jacobs felt like the shit was finally starting to hit the fan. He knew he'd pissed off a lot of big hats down at headquarters and the third precinct – but he was doing what he loved. He was willing to live with it, and by all means, he wanted his son to live out his purpose. He knew Antwan bled blue just like he did, but it was no way he was going to allow him to be lied to and misguided by anyone. He'd made up his mind that he would reveal to him just how corrupt the LAPD was.

Antwan was having the time of his life. After the second pint of Hennessy kicked in, the girls began giving lap dances. Perkins began passing everyone imported Cuban cigars. Then, he invited Antwan over to the gun range.

"I heard you're a great shot."

"Yeah! I do a little something!" he replied, loading his service weapon, while Perkins began setting up the target.

Even under the influence of alcohol, Antwan shot exceptionally well. Perkins was impressed, but as soon as he observed Antwan put his weapon down to go and use the restroom, he switched his and replaced it with another. Antwan returned and began shooting as if nothing happened. Minutes later, a call from border control came across their radios. It was time to load up and head out.

Antwan looked up at Perkins and said, "I've had a little too much to drink, Captain."

"Shit, we all have," Perkins replied as the entire room filled with laughter.

"I feel as though I would be doing more harm than good. It's obvious that I'm too impaired to drive. It's a death sentence for me to search the Mojave desert with a gun and a vest looking for illegal immigrants who might have guns and crossing the border at night. Respectfully, Captain, give me a pass, please." Perkins nodded in agreeance and he and the other officers began exiting the building.

Antwan sat in deep thought, contemplating his next move. As he sat looking up at the ceiling, he thought about how this was the complete opposite of what he had always envisioned his career to be.

❖

Kelly was sitting in the back drinking when Captain Perkins introduced Antwan Jacobs to the unit. He didn't feel it was even necessary to introduce himself, knowing he would probably be the person killing him eventually. He sat back while reminiscing about his recent run-in with his father at his residence. Wishing he had just jumped out shooting. He was starting to get tired of tailing and surveillance.
He could care less about a meet and greet. If it were up to him, he would take Antwan behind the warehouse and shoot him right in his head. So, he decided to keep his distance, but he did notice one thing about Antwan. He was very observant, and he knew he was being watched.

Detective Jacobs didn't want Ranson to have any links to his whereabouts, especially where he rested his head. His realtor, Alex Applegate, continued to press him about certain properties he had available, but he had his own plans in mind. *Ranson wouldn't get the drop on this location,* he said to himself.

Montana was an amazing place to live. Often, Detective Jacobs reminisced of the good times he'd spent there teaching his son survival skills. He was confident Antwan could survive a full week off the grid alone. Snapping out of his daydream, Detective Jacobs walked into the Montana relator's office. This was the first step to purchasing the house of his dreams. It was only a matter of time before he could retire and enjoy

the rest of his life by fishing and hunting. First, he had
to complete the mission he started.

Chapter 4
The Cartel

It was a bright and sunny California day when Antwan received a text from his father with instructions to meet him at the Burbank International Private Airport, but he had no clue he would be taking a flight. He arrived on time just to see his father loading up the last of the luggage along with the pilot doing his mandatory maintenance check.

"Son!! Happy to see you made it."

"Dad, where are we going?"

"Montana. I have something I want you to see. I figured we could fly out for a couple of hours and be back home by midafternoon."

"Sounds like a plan to me," Antwan replied, entering the private jet.

He loved everything about Montana. His father had taught him so much up in the mountains since he was a kid. Going to Montana was always a grand affair and a trip he would never turn down, but little did he know this would be a different trip to Montana than any of his previous visits.

Just outside of the airport, parked in his SUV, Kelly sat pondering, trying to figure out just how he was going to persuade the flight personnel to tell him where Detective Jacobs' flight had taken off to.

You would have thought the first couple of hours on the jet would be exciting. Yet, after Antwan and his father finished their breakfast, they both slept the entire flight. Detective Jacobs was catching up on some well-needed rest. Ever since his home had been broken into, he hadn't slept much. Antwan hadn't been resting either. He wasn't feeling his new promotion and was almost ready to quit. He grew up seeing law enforcement in a much different light then what was being presented to him. The Unit 12 special weapons and tactical team looked more like rappers and ballplayer's than the LAPD.

The energy Antwan received from Unit 12, all the way up to the administration, was negative and unbalanced, and it made him feel uncomfortable. He didn't want to mention it to his father, thinking he would take it as him being ungrateful. So, he decided to keep his promotion to himself.

Ranson, Chief Lewis, and Captain Perkins were all in a Zoom meeting discussing the situation at hand.

"We went ahead and promoted his son, Antwan Jacobs, with hopes that would have Detective Jacobs pump his breaks for the time being. It seems as if he's still adamant about exposing us to internal affairs."

41

Little did they know, Detective Jacobs was weeks away from doing what he was sent out to do. He just had to have this important meeting with his son.

Kelly the Killer......

"Yes -," he said proudly with authority, "I'm his partner of ten years. Detective Willie Waverly is the name," he said while flashing his detective badge and fake identification.

The clerk suddenly stopped typing, looked up, and said, "The information we have in our database says confidential, but what I can tell you is that his flight will be landing shortly, and when it does, I can have my business associate relay your message to him," she said while looking down at her computer screen.

"Is there a supervisor present that I can speak to? This is vital law enforcement information he needs."

"No!" she replied with a slight attitude, as if she was starting to get annoyed. "My supervisor is unavailable. She's out for lunch and won't be returning for another hour or two. I'm the only person here at the moment. Mr. Jacobs has his information flagged in our system as confidential, and I'm not loosing my job for nobody."

Kelly looked around and noticed that there weren't any cameras in the office. He exited outside to see if there were any by the main entrance. After shockingly discovering that, in 2024, there were no cameras, he walked out of the building over to his

42

squad car, put on a pair of gloves, and headed back into the office. The clerk was still standing by her computer when he entered the office.

Montana, Montana...

"Man, look how amazing this place is Dad," Antwan said, admiring the snow on top of the mountains as they began unloading his father's luggage. "It's so peaceful and beautiful out here. Dad did you know conspiracy theorists say that mountains are actually dead giants and tree stomps?"

"Trees and giants, son? Man, you got to stay off of that internet weed," Detective Jacobs said, laughing.

"No Dad, for real – think about this. We've had previous conversations about you believing that giants did roam the earth at one time, correct?"

"Agreed!" his father replied, "but that was back in the biblical days of David and Goliath, son."

"Okay, they say some giants were as tall as twenty feet, correct?"

"Yes, that's correct, son. The only giant, on record, that I know of is Robert Wadlow. He was eight feet, eleven inches when he died son."

"Dad, the average tree is twenty-five feet. Giants had to have trees to sit under, too! These beautiful mountains we're looking at could be the stumps or the giants that once existed. You have to stay woke, Dad."

"I'm going to have to do some woke research on that. You pulled that one out of a hat," Detective Jacobs said, laughing. "In the meantime, grab this bag and this suitcase."

"These bags are heavy as hell," Antwan said, while walking them over to their awaiting Yukon Denali.

The clerk looked up, and within a matter of seconds, he'd dived across the counter and began choking her. Then, he smacked her several times and made her pull up the flight reservations and destination route for Detective Jacobs.

After she retrieved the confidential information, Kelly proceeded to shoot her point blank in her head, killing her instantly. He noticed that Jacobs' flight log revealed that he'd taken several flights from Los Angeles to Montana in the past 90 days. *It looks like I'll be taking a flight,* he said to himself as he continued to write down the information on the computer.

"Home sweet home," Detective Jacobs said, entering his massive estate. "I can't wait to retire, so I can enjoy this amazing view," he said, looking out at the famous Montana Granite Peak mountains. "Grab a couple of bags and follow me, son. I have something I want to show you."

They exited the back of the estate and went into his enormously huge backyard. Detective Jacobs began pacing fifteen meters forward and five meters to the right, and there, under his right foot, was a piece of artificial turf that seemed to have blended in very well with the rest of the landscaping.

After pulling the turf up, it revealed a long chain. He pulled it, and to Antwan's amazement, he watched as a secret door opened with steps going down at least a hundred feet below.

"This right here, son, is our underground bunker. It has a blast-resistant door with electrical plumbing and a top-of-the-line ventilation system with air filtration. This bunker is huge and can sustain up to twenty-five people for up to five years."

Antwan looked on in amazement. "It's actually an underground home," he said, walking around, switching the lights on and off while opening up the refrigerator. Does this phone even work, Dad?"

"Of course, everything does, including the computers in the media room."

"I can see myself living down here for real, Dad."

Back at headquarters...

"Talk to me," Captain Perkins said, answering his cell phone.

"I tracked down Detective Jacobs and discovered he's been taking a lot of flights to Montana recently," Kelly said. "Things got a little out of control, and I had to get messy on my end."

"Well, you know, in our line of work, most of the time, that's necessary!" Perkins replied, knowing if Kelly said it like that, he'd probably killed someone. "Get back to headquarters as soon as you can. I'm going to inform Ranson of your progress. I know he will be ecstatic to hear the intel you've discovered."

"That's a 10-4, Captain," Kelly said before ending his call.

Captain Perkins hung up feeling a lot better. It had been well over a month without a solid lead on Jacobs. Now, it was time to put the pressure on. Things had gotten so bad that he couldn't move a nickel bag in the park if he wanted to! Thanks to Jacobs, everything was at a standstill. Ranson was losing customers and millions of dollars by the day. Even some of his most dedicated clients on the black market were starting to get irritated and impatient.

The underground bunker...

"This is what I wanted to talk to you about," Detective Jacobs said as he opened the massive walk-in safe. It held over half a million dollars in currency, guns, and cocaine. "These drugs, guns, and money you're looking at don't belong to me. I was placed as a mole, and I confiscated it as evidence against Ranson and his corrupt unit. Now, this is going to bring down some big hat officials on the police force. So, I'm going to need you to be aware of what's going on because your life could be at risk as well.

46

From this point on, you will have to move cautiously, be alert, and watch the cops in your company – don't trust them. Nine times out of ten, they're working for Ranson. I plan on giving all of this evidence to the federal authorities back in Virginia. There's no way, I'm trusting any other cop, especially from the LAPD. I even have a funny feeling about Bo Rodgers down at the federal headquarters. He's been acting strange, and that's unlike him. Then again, he has always been motivated by money. I wouldn't be surprised if he and Ranson were in cahoots. You can't trust anyone from our district with a badge. So, If anything happens to me –"

"But nothing will! Antwan quickly interrupted.

"Listen to me, son. I need you to stay focused and listen. Like I was saying, if anything should happen to me, this is the person I need for you to give all of this evidence to. He will know how to handle it from there. I'm sorry you had to be a part of this, but it's just the right thing to do!" Detective Jacobs said as he walked back up the stairs, leaving Antwan stuck in his thoughts.

Antwan looked down and opened the black suitcase. It revealed several kilos of cocaine. Each brick came with a scorpion stamp placed in the middle. From his police training, he realized that it was the official stamp of one of the most feared cartels on the planet, The Sinaloa Cartel. They were known for torturing and murdering couriers who failed to deliver on time and whomever stood in the way of their drug trade. He proceeded to open the second bag. It revealed a substantial amount of currency. Stuck in his thoughts, Antwan looked down at the piece of paper his father gave to him.

It read,

Private investigator, Anthony Hayes, Internal Affairs

Antwan made note of it by putting the information into his phone. He never had the opportunity to tell his father he'd recently just been assigned to Unit 12, but now everything was starting to make sense.

We go way back...

Anthony L. Hayes and Dwayne Jacobs were best friends and had been partners on the force for more than twelve years. They joined together in 2000 as rookies and eventually worked their way through the rankings, becoming two of the top-ranking detectives in their division.

Eventually, Jacobs would get the opportunity to have his own twelve-man swat unit, along with a $120k annual salary, and an unmarked police vehicle. All were available to him upon his transfer from the robbery division. He gladly accepted and left his division that following week. Anthony Hayes would retire and eventually join the internal affairs federal response team. This time, he was linking up with Detective Jacobs to bring down the notorious Brock Ranson and his corrupt police unit. Little did Ranson

48

know, the Sinaloa Cartel had been onto his tactical team, taking their drugs and reselling them back to organized street gangs throughout the United States.

They were fully aware of the murders and robberies, but they didn't want to push the issue. Only because, for every truckload of cocaine that was intercepted by Unit 12, twenty-five truckloads would make it across the border. They looked at it as if they were just paying their taxes, but eventually, they had every intention to retaliate.

After he'd strangled and killed the clerk, Kelly wrapped her body in several trash bags. He proceeded to drag her body to one of the older broken-down planes he knew wouldn't be used. Then, he jumped in the nearest airplane and headed straight to Jacobs' location. Kelly arrived in Montana around mid-afternoon. He had Detective Jacobs' phone location locked into his GPS, and now he could ping his exact location.

While driving in deep thought, Kelly contemplated his next move. He drove for approximately twenty minutes until he noticed a small convenience store and gas station. He drove up and decided to grab a snack and some gas. The store was almost completely empty when he entered. To his immediate left, he noticed two people talking by the soda machine, and another older woman was eating a sandwich while playing a scratch-off lottery ticket.

"Good evening ladies! My name is William Waverly. I'm traveling from California. Is it possible that you can direct me to a hotel or motel? Are there any diners or restaurants near where I can relax and enjoy a good meal?"

"Oh no," the older woman replied. "This is the only gas station and store in this area for miles. The restaurants are all in town."

"And which way is that?" He asked.

"You're going to have to turn around, get back on I-90, and head north for about twenty to twenty-five miles. While you are driving, you will begin to see signs and exit markers that say food, lodging, and gas. Take the first exit, which should be thirteen. You will come up to an intersection, and the shopping center should be directly to your right. It's plenty of restaurants there you can eat at."

"Thank you," Kelly said, getting back into his vehicle.

He knew, at that moment, he was in the right area because his pings would only hit if he was within a 1–50-mile radius and this was the only convenience store and gas station for the next twenty miles. He sat parked and surveillance the entire area. He was confident he would be seeing Detective Jacobs soon.

The luxury estates and gated communities just up the road had him thinking that, just maybe, Detective Jacobs was living closer than he thought. Five hours, three chili dogs, and two beers later, two pings on his phone alerted him. That's when he knew Detective Jacobs was close.

Detective Jacobs and Antwan were, in fact, five minutes away at the Fresh Bait and Tackle store. They decided to go freshwater fly fishing down on the Yellow Stone River. It had been a lot to take in the past couple of weeks, so it was time to hit the reset button from all the turmoil that had been going on. Dwayne also felt that Antwan deserved to hear how and why all of this was happening.

Patience is truly a virtue because Kelly followed his gut and laid at the convenience store. He couldn't believe it when he observed Jacobs pulling in. He quickly slumped in his seat while he drove past and parked by the gas pump. His opportunity came when they both exited and entered the store. He timed them perfectly as he walked alongside Jacobs' vehicle so that he could place a tracking device just above the back passenger wheel. Then, he turned around to get back into his vehicle and exit the gas station as fast as possible. He couldn't wait to call Ranson with the great news.

"So basically, you were placed in Unit 12 as a mole to do an internal investigation this entire time?" Antwan asked.

"Yes, I had to play a part in getting Ranson to finally trust me. He knew if he could get me to go along with him, nobody in law enforcement would see anything he was doing as corrupt. So yes, I was the mole planted to infiltrate Unit 12, so that Ranson could carry out his destructive agenda. Sometimes, no matter the role I was playing, I couldn't fake half the shit I was witnessing. My morality could never match their energy, and I know, for sure, they felt it. As my mission completes, the pressure is on because a lot of big hats in law enforcement are going down along with Ranson, including Unit 12." Dwayne noticed a sudden change in his son, "What's wrong?"

Antwan looked up at his father and finally said, "Dad, I was just promoted to Unit 12 three weeks ago!"

Chapter 5
The Mojave Border

Captain Perkins and Unit 12 were closing in on another big load from intel suspected of having over ten million dollars in US currency. They sat, patiently waiting. Thirty minutes later, a charter bus pulled in full of immigrants. The driver said they were on their way to Nevada and everyone on his bus had their legal documents to enter the United States.

Perkins wasn't trying to hear any of what he had to say. So, one-by-one, he had every passenger escorted off of the bus by gunpoint. It was then they were searched and detained.

"The cartel is not going to like this!" Officer Williams said.

He was aware that they didn't care about the load getting confiscated. He knew it was all a part of their elaborate plan to get the rest of their shipments through. He and Perkins both walked around to the side of the charter bus, and there sat a shipment of over two hundred illegal, brand-new United States Army AR-15 and AK-47 assault rifles.

"No money?" Perkins asked.

"As of now, no. We'll probably have to take the bus back to headquarters and dismantle it piece by piece. I'm pretty sure the cartel utilized as much space as they could."

"This could turn ugly," Williams said, walking up on their conversation.

"I'm just following Captain Ranson's orders," Perkins replied. "Everyone, gather up and take these immigrants to the back of the bus and kill them. Williams, you drive the bus back to headquarters. I'll have Quinn and Mayes escort you there."

Perkins and the rest of the unit stayed back. In all, they killed a total of twenty-two men and released the women and children. Officer Williams knew the cartel was watching from a distance, and they were sure to retaliate. He just didn't know how, when, or where, but he felt it coming.

"Three weeks ago!?! My goodness!! Who in their right mind would assign you to a unit that's currently under federal investigation!?"

"Deputy Chief Lewis, 3rd precinct," Antwan replied.

"Yeah, you're not going back there. This was an elaborate plan that was thought out, conspired, and orchestrated by, none other than, Brock Ranson himself."

Immediately, Detective Jacobs called internal affairs, Norfolk VA division, to speak with his friend Anthony Hayes. Jacobs asked if Antwan could get an emergency transfer from the third precinct.

"That shouldn't be a problem," Hayes replied. "I'll get on top of it."

Detective Jacobs hung up. He sat in shock, thinking of how much of a dirty game Ranson was playing by recruiting Antwan and making him a part of the Unit 12 conspiracy. *He probably figured that, if he added Antwan to the investigation, I would no longer pursue them,* he thought as he began walking back into his massive great room where Antwan was sitting. He sat down beside him, and told him for his safety, that he'd put in an emergency transfer for him to another jurisdiction outside of Los Angeles.

Meanwhile, the tracking device installed on Detective Jacobs' vehicle led Kelly fifteen minutes out of the city. Kelly was there, outside of the residence, lurking and scoping the scene. Jacobs' estate was private property, so Kelly had to park his vehicle almost 300 yards away and walk up a dirt hill full of wild trees and bushes. He sat and took pictures of the elegant estate, still not knowing if this was just an Airbnb or his actual residence. He also took notice of the high-tech surveillance motion detectors, flood lights, and the Bose bull horn he noticed on top of the roof. When sounding, it's alarm could wake up the entire city. With this much security, he was convinced this had to be his residence.

Back in La, Antwan and Officer Gomez were scheduled to meet up. It seemed as if his days were flying by, and it was already time for turn-up Tuesdays. He had literally flown away just for the weekend, spending time with his father in Montana. He arrived to the Buffalo Wild Wings around nine-thirty and noticed her right away. Not because of her outfit, but because she was the sexiest woman in the restaurant.

Damn! Is this all you? he asked himself, looking at her voluptuous body.

"Yeah, I told you I look good outside of my work clothes," she responded.

"Yes! You absolutely do. Can't hide all that azz if you tried," Antwan replied, giving her a long-awaited hug and kiss.

Their evening went exceptionally well. They laughed and reminisced about their first domestic disturbance call. "You handled it very professionally and with poise and authority. It was sexy to me," she complimented.

"I appreciate that, Gomez," Antwan replied while paying the waitress for their meal.

"And from this point on can you do me a favor, please?"

"Of course! Anything!" he said, holding her small, soft hands, while looking into her beautiful hazel eyes.

56

"Just call me, Veronica."

"I can most definitely do that," he replied, smiling from ear to ear.

Detective Jacobs was back on the job talking to another detective that he didn't trust as far as he could throw him. At this point, in his eyes, everyone wearing blue with badges were all corrupt. His internal investigation was complete. He had enough evidence on Ranson to put him and the entire unit under the prison. *Just a week away from retirement, and this nightmare of a career will be over,* he thought to himself.

Already dressed in his S.W.A.T tactical gear, Jacobs received the call over his radio that rapid gunfire was being exchanged just off of Interstate I-90. Police backup had been requested immediately and the chief of police came over dispatch to call for all hands on deck. Detective Jacobs was within earshot and called it in.

Antwan was within ten miles of the scene and he heard the call. Even though he wasn't a third precinct officer anymore, he'd still sworn to protect and serve. After hearing his father's response over the radio, he activated his siren, placed his blue police light into his windshield, and headed over to the location as fast as he could.

The Sinaloa cartel had struck again and this time they had several regular police officers duck-taped and tied up. The last load of assault weapons the unit took from the cartel didn't sit well with them, and they wanted the people responsible along with their guns and money. When Detective Jacobs arrived, it was twenty-five masked cartel members standing alongside LAPD holdings assault rifles.

He noticed the situation at first glance and realized that he was set up and blindsided by his own unit. All of a sudden, two sprint vans drove up fast and blocked his vehicle from behind. Detective Jacobs observed several short Mexican men wearing charro hats and cowboy boots, all standing alongside Captain Perkins. Perkins pointed towards Detective Jacobs and he was removed from his vehicle by gunpoint, instantly. Once out he was ordered to get down on his knees. Their Jefe walked over and asked him where was his drug shipment, money, and guns.

Deep down Detective Jacobs knew it was over for him. He told the Jefe it was now in the hands of the United States Federal government. Without further ado, Perkins passed the Jefe Antwan's service weapon as he proceeded to shoot him point blank in the back of his head. Antwan drove up at the very moment that it was happening, witnessing his father getting shot, point blank range, as his body flopped to the ground.

The first person who recognized him was Captain Perkins. He put his car in reverse and backed his hellcat out as fast as he could, taking on a full assault of bullets. Fortunately, he managed to get away with his life, but he couldn't stop crying. How could he lie after he'd just witnessed his own father's execution? His superhero was no longer here to show him the ropes, or give him advice. Now, his only mission was to honor what his father believed in. He backed his riddled-up vehicle into his storage unit, then proceeded to cover it with a blue tarp. He walked from out of the facility with one mission, and that was to bring Ranson, Captain Perkins, and his entire Unit 12 to justice.

He just had to get the evidence to investigator Anthony Hayes in Virginia. By the time Antwan entered back into LA County, he'd heard the emergency call over the airway that he'd just shot and killed his father, Detective Jacobs, and was last seen driving eastbound on I-90.

Every unit was given a "Be On The Look Out" (BOLO) for a dark blue 2024 SRT hellcat, and told the subject was to be considered armed and dangerous. Antwan knew the first thing he had to do was ditch his vehicle. So, he had Veronica meet him at the McDonald's two blocks away from the storage. It was there in the parking lot where he told her the entire story.

She sat and listened as if he was quoting a Jeremy Jae-Jae Davis, New York Times best seller. They had to get out of California as soon as possible. The BOLO went out to every transportation service in the states of California and Nevada. Two hours into their drive, they finally heard the false allegations and details of the crime.

Several witnesses stated that Antwan and his father got into a heated argument. Allegedly, the two got into a scuffle, leaving Antwan gasping for air while lying on the ground. Detective Jacobs walked away from the confrontation to enter his vehicle, and that's when his son, Antwan, walked up from behind and shot him point blank in the back of his head. Antwan Jacobs' police service weapon was recovered at the scene and has been reported by forensics as the murder weapon. Several officers in Unit 12 made statements and were ready to testify to what they witnessed. An autopsy was ordered immediately.

"What the hell!? But how?"

Antwan pulled out his service weapon and checked the serial number. Officers at the academy were taught to memorize everything about their service weapons, especially the serial numbers. He noticed it was a completely different gun. "Man, these cops are fuckin criminals. Chief Lewis, down to Captain Perkins are all on Brock Ranson's payroll. They were setting me up the entire time!"

Chapter 6
Heaven on Earth

The estate was immaculate. He could see why his father called it his heaven on earth. The Montana Ridge estate was paradise in the mountains. Antwan figured he and Veronica could lay low just until he got everything lined up. Every news station showcased his portfolio several times, labeling him the cop killer. After taking two Advil, he laid back on the couch, shut his eyes, and relaxed. He'd been through a lot of stress the past twenty-four hours. He suddenly felt a presence in the room he was in.

When he opened his eyes, to his surprise, Veronica was standing in front of him completely naked. Her voluptuous body looked amazing! Suddenly, his headache mysteriously disappeared. Without hesitation, he scooped her off of her feet and began walking her into the adjacent bedroom where they both did what they had been waiting to do for a long time.

Antwan woke up feeling like a rejuvenated man. Clearly, that was all the aspirin he needed. However, he knew he would have to get the evidence. So, he decided not to go near the bunker unless he was clearing it out. He didn't want to expose it. He had to come up with a safe and efficient evacuation route because every cop on the West Coast was out looking for him.

Back at headquarters...

Upon further investigation, the detectives went over the video footage and were able to track Antwan down using satellite imagery, tracking his GPS to his Dodge Challenger. Two hours and fourteen minutes later, his storage unit was raided by federal agents only to discover his riddled-up, dismantled vehicle. Ranson had the judge issue a no-knock warrant, allowing officials to search every address, hotel, or family member's residence in the state of California, who they felt could be harboring their fugitive.

Fortunately for Antwan, it was just him and his father. His mother had passed away twenty-two years ago and now the same people he looked up and dedicated his life and service to were all back at headquarters signing his death certificate. He knew he had to move and move fast.

Antwan woke up around 2 am. He walked out onto the balcony to get some well-needed fresh air. That's when he noticed a small dim light coming from what looked to be a vehicle parked about a hundred yards away. *This is private property, no car should have been within five hundred yards*, he said to himself. He walked back into the estate and quickly got dressed. Then, he exited through the back door, but not before retrieving his night vision binoculars and his AR-15 assault rifle. Upon looking into the binoculars, he noticed that it was Ranson's biggest flunkie, Officer Kelly.

"Shit!" he yelled, knowing that if Kelly was sent, it was to only do one thing, and that was kill him. Luckily, he knew he had the ups on Kelly, Antwan thought to himself, before grabbing an extra cartridge of bullets. He exited the estate fully dressed in black army fatigues and body armor. As soon as he arrived at the hill, he quietly scaled down like a thief in the night.

Upon approaching, he noticed that Kelly was looking down at his computer monitor. He had just caught his killer slipping. He ambushed him, pointing his AR-15 directly to the window. Kelly was obviously shaken up, so Antwan calmly instructed him to put both hands on top of the steering wheel. "One false move, and I promise I'm going to blow out every little piece of brain you have left in your cranium."

Kelly complied while laughing, "You're one bold kid," he said, "but it is rules to engagement, and you definitely have the upper hand. I'm going to have to eat this one. No matter what you do to me, your bitch ass is still going to die, and if we don't kill you here, your black azz is going to die in that electric chair for capital murder! You think you're safe and out the way hiding out in Montana? The entire LAPD is looking for your azz. To put the icing on the cake, I've already sent out your sweet location."

Those words cut through him like a hot knife. Antwan loved the shield the same way his father had and could have never imagined being called a cop

63

killer. He bled blue and took an oath to serve and to protect. "I've never been that!" Antwan yelled. "Until now...

Boom, Boom, Boom!

Antwan looked down at the monitor and read the conversation that Kelly was having. In fact, he had given out his location to Brock Ranson. He hurried back to the estate. Once there, he entered the master bedroom and noticed Veronica still asleep. He immediately woke her, telling her she had to get up and leave right away.

"What's wrong baby?"

"Our location has been compromised, and it's no telling how much time we have left before the estate gets raided."

Barely dressed, Veronica picked up her clothes and heels from the floor and quickly followed behind him. Once downstairs, Antwan passed her the keys to his father's vehicle. "I'm going to need for you to keep calling this number until you get an answer. It's the phone number to the internal affairs lead investigator, Anthony Hayes. Let him know that Unit 12 is en route to my location to try and retrieve the missing federal evidence that I have against them. So, I'm going to need for him to get here as soon as he can. Also, let him know about the bunker just in case he arrives and can't find me."

"Please be careful," she said, standing on her toes to give him a kiss.

"I will!"

Veronica left the estate through the back exit while Antwan stood and watched as she drove away, disappearing into the night. Antwan was in full go mode now that Veronica was out of harm's way. He immediately ran back down into the bunker and began loading up his arsenal of weapons. He'd grown up in these wooded mountains of Montana and pretty much knew the terrain better than the average person residing there. He knew his chances of survival were greater if he left the estate and set up camp somewhere in the woods that he grew up playing in throughout his adolescent years. So, he sat and strategically put his master plan in motion.

Veronica was twenty-five miles down the road. The thought of boarding an airplane without her man was absolutely absurd. She'd actually checked into the local Days Inn downtown. Once settled, she began calling a few of her connections in Great Falls, Montana, and California, informing them of the situation and its entirety.

Back in LA...

"We are live at the LAPD headquarters. We have just received updated information about the killing of a twenty-year detective on the force. Our sources revealed that Captain Dwayne Jacobs was allegedly shot and killed by his son Antwan Jacobs, a rookie on the force. He is now wanted for questioning. Police officials are telling us his whereabouts are unknown at this time. If you or anyone else has seen

65

this suspect, call 911. Please do not approach. He is considered to be armed and dangerous. I'm here with Captain Brock Ranson and Chief Lewis of the third precinct. Is there any new information that the public should be aware of?"

Chief Lewis stepped up and approached the podium. "We will be updating you as soon as we receive it. Right now, our suspect is believed to be traveling alone. He was last seen traveling eastbound in a dark blue Dodge Challenger with dark-tinted windows, exiting the city of Los Angeles. We have our federal and state law enforcement officials looking into this investigation thoroughly. After we gather all of the evidence, we will be back updating the public soon."

"That was Deputy Chief Lewis of the third division precinct. Now, back to our studio. I'm Karen Myers, reporting live for WLAC-13 on your side."

Back at the border, Captain Perkins and his unit were all gearing up to make the two-hour flight to Montana. Ranson had the official blueprint of Dwayne's estate and hurried to email it to Perkins. Unaware of the added underground bunker that was recently installed. Meanwhile, Antwan was in the forest setting up landmines, and trip wires with grenades attached, and man death holes.

He was determined to use every element of the forest in his favor. He knew that nature was definitely on his side. Within a matter of minutes, it became extremely windy and rainy, giving him the upper hand against his opposition.

Back at headquarters, Chief Deputy Lewis and the infamous Bo Rodgers were together on a conference call with Ranson, discussing how critical their mission was. Ranson was adamant about Antwan being captured alive in hopes that he would give up the evidence he had against them, and if everything was to play out in their favor, he would never make it to trial. He would be executed as soon as the evidence was discovered. Ranson sat at his desk and smoked a cigar, patiently waiting to hear back from the unit.

Antwan finally heard back from Special Agent Hayes. "Hello Antwan, I'm glad we finally have the opportunity to talk. A young lady by the name of Veronica Gomez has been calling me nonstop since yesterday and leaving messages for me to call you as soon as possible."

"Yeah, that's my girlfriend," Antwan replied. "My father said not to trust anyone but you for some reason."

Agent Hayes laughed, "He has a good reason to," he responded. "I saved your father's life twice while working the robbery division. We were two peas in the pod – thick as thieves – and best friends for over two decades. I'm honored that he said that. I'm really going to miss him, and I'm going to do everything in my power to bring the people responsible for his death to justice. The question is, what do you have for me?"

❖

The private plane was fully occupied. All twelve were wearing ski masks while holding their AR-15 assault rifles. Captain Perkins stood up to address the unit and went over the plans for the final time. "Listen, we are here to capture and detain Jacobs. Our orders are to bring him to Perkins alive. It's no telling where he has hidden the evidence, so we are going to have to tear every inch of his estate to scrap metal. Leave no stone unturned."

"Ten-four!!" they all said in unison.

"I will also have two units searching a two-acre perimeter of the Yellow Stone forest and river. Agent McNair will be flying the helicopter. He will be our eye in the sky. We're not anticipating Jacobs to be present at the estate upon arrival. Remember, you must 12-40 and ask permission to shoot before engaging. Keep your radios on channel three and your earbuds in. I've just been informed that he is very familiar with the surrounding terrain, so stay alert and vigilant at all times."

"My goodness!" Special Agent Hayes replied. "You have all of that hidden in an underground bunker that's not on the registered city blueprint?"

"That's correct," Antwan replied. "My father had it added months ago and he never had clearance from the city to build it. He told me he'd hired out-of-state contractors for the job. Inside, it's at least a truckload of cocaine, guns, United States currency, wiretaps, and everything you alphabet boys love giving out indictments for. My time is limited because they are en route to retrieve the evidence and kill me."

"Well, I'll be damned!" Agent Hayes responded. "I should have known Dwayne would have his ducks in a row. That's just the kind of detective he was. Okay, I'm going to give your statement to my superiors and once they okay it, the judge will sign the warrants, and I should have a federal tactical team headed to Montana within the next twenty-four hours. I believe it would be safer if you stayed inside of the bunker until we arrived, correct?" Agent Hayes suggested.

"Yeah, I can do that!" Antwan replied, while loading his M-4 Smith-n-Wesson assault riffle.

Agent Hayes's tripping, he thought to himself. There was no way he was going to just sit and wait to be rescued. He was determined to catch a couple of bodies. He wasn't going out like no tinder dick, especially not after what they did to his father.

"My code word is Sunny Side Drive. So, if you hear me say that over the bullhorn, then it's safe for you to exit."

"I got it. I'll see you in twenty-four hours.'

"Stay safe!" Agent Hayes said before hanging up.

Antwan hung up and began walking towards the edge of the hill. He couldn't imagine being anywhere else at this moment. The Montana mountain scenery was just that amazing to witness, but the weather wasn't getting any better. The forecast called for strong, high wind gusts at fifteen miles an hour. The added precipitation, made it difficult to see clearly. The lone warrior stood tall, soaking it all in, in preparation for the one-man battle he was about to embark on.

Back at headquarters, Ranson received a call from Bo Rodgers. "This is Ranson!"

"It's not looking good, sir. Usually, I could take over any case, but internal affairs have taken over this investigation. What we have is a crucial twelve-hour window to get into Jacobs' estate, find the evidence, and get the hell out of Montana as fast as we can before the alphabet boys arrive!"

"That's cutting it, but I guess we have to work with what we have," Ranson replied, trying not to sound like his usual arrogant self. "Please, don't allow any officers to get caught outside of your jurisdiction. If so, it will validate everything Jacobs is claiming to be true."

"That's a ten-four," Ranson replied before hanging up.

He knew his back was against the wall, and not only would he go down for his crimes, but the entire third precinct would, including Chief Lewis.

Ranson called Perkins with the updated information.

The two-hour flight landed at the Great Falls International Airport around noon. The first unit of officers exited the plane and began loading into both caravans that were headed towards Jacobs' estate. The other twelve were arriving by boat. Perkins looked at his watch, anticipating the other twelve to arrive around the same time. Their mission was to get in, recover the evidence, and exit the property expeditiously. Their window of opportunity was beginning to narrow down.

The execution of this mission was pivotal. Not only was time not on their side, but their livelihoods and careers were on the line as well. Several officers were equipped with body cameras, allowing Ranson to have a first-hand look at what was happening in real-time. This allowed him to be able to call orders if necessary. By the time they reach the estate, their caravan suddenly began to take on rapid gunfire. All they could do was pull over, exit, and retreat to a safer spot.

Antwan was upset that he'd missed them because that was a rare occurrence. He had to keep in mind that trying to hit a moving vehicle with the rain and high wind gusts blowing in his face was challenging. He quickly retreated to another location on top of the hill. It was there where he held the advantage of blending in with the surrounding terrain. He looked down from his vantage point and began shooting at any and everything he observed moving on his property.

Perkins and several other officers took cover behind the van, while Antwan let off a relentless amount of firepower. Captain Perkins listened carefully. He knew for sure that Jacobs was shooting a AR-15, and he was going to need to reload. As soon as the barrage of bullets ceased, Captain Perkins began shooting back up the hill toward Antwan, allowing his officers to take cover in various locations.

Antwan knew exactly what they were doing because he was trained to do the exact thing. He knew eventually, he would run out of time and would probably end up dying, but he promised himself if that were to happen, he was going to take as many with him as he could. The second unit arrived by boat. They exited and were ready to go into full combat mode with their arsenal of weapons. Little did they know, Antwan was prepared for that also. The day before, he spent diligent hours strategically scattering IED land mines along the beach.

After he finally stopped shooting at Perkins and his unit, he heard two explosions coming from the east end of his property. He knew the water unit had arrived. He quickly retreated into the forest, knowing that if he took his fight there, his chances of survival were greater.

The communication between the units became chaotic due to multiple officers yelling into their radios at the same time. In total, there were three injuries and one fatality stemming from the officer stepping on top of the landmine. The remaining officers stood frightened, not wanting to move another step forward. So, for safety precautions, they each backtracked their way back to their boat.

Then, Perkins instructed two officers to stay back with the injured officers. He was now operating an eight-man unit. He instructed his driver to head up the river. Unfortunately, the high tide, along with the rain and windy forecast, was going to set them back thirty to forty minutes.

Brock Ranson looked on in shock! It had already been over an hour and Jacobs still hadn't been captured by his most skilled combat unit by far. *This was absurd,* he thought to himself as he looked down at his Rolex.

Perkins radioed in, confirming to Ranson that both units would be zeroing in within the next thirty minutes. Meanwhile, Ranson had assigned four officers to tear the lavish 6,500 square-foot estate to ruins. They tore holes into the walls, floors, and ceilings, leaving no stone unturned.

Yellow Stone National Forest...

Antwan was resting on top of a Menziesii oak tree. It's one of the tallest trees in Yellow Stone – just on of the many facts his father taught him. He quietly sat, looking down at Ranson's entire operation taking place. Disguised in army camouflage, he blended in naturally with his surroundings. He watched as the group of officers walked past, headed in the direction he'd just left. He was just about to scale down the tree when he noticed a loner about two meters behind the group. This had been the opportunity he was waiting for. He pulled a rock from out of his pocket along with his bow and arrow.

Then, he proceeded to drop the rock, hitting the leaves directly in front of the officer. As soon as he heard it, out of instinct, he looked up, only to meet his demise with an arrow penetrating straight through his skull. Antwan scaled down the enormous tree and began stripping the officer of his radio, uniform, and tactical gear, before covering him with leaves. Now, he was equipped with everything he needed to fight against Unit 12. So, instead of just listening, he spoke on the radio.

"Ranson, I'm coming to get your azz!"

"Jacobs? Is that you? I'm surprised you're still breathing. I strongly suggest that if you want it to remain that way, immediately drop your weapons and surrender. Either way, you're leaving this mountain top with us by choice or by force. On your own or in a body bag."

Antwan burst out laughing over the radio. "Listen to me, you scumbag! I'm not surrendering to no cop killers from the LAPD. I promise you, at first chance, I'm going to personally put a bullet in both of your heads. You drew first blood Ranson, and I'm here to reap havoc."

Antwan's initial goal was to cut the communication barrier between the officers. He knew that, without proper communication, they would eventually have to abort the mission. Luckily for him, not only did he know his terrain, but he also knew Unit 12's tactics on how they moved and executed their raids. This gave him a greater advantage while leaving Ranson stuck in his thoughts.

"Perkins, you copy?" Ranson asked.

"Copy sir!" he responded.

"Our radios have been compromised. So, you're going to have to move by instinct and skill. Get Jacobs to me! I don't care how. He can be in a body bag for all I care. Just bring him to me and abort all radio communication."

"That's a ten-four, Captain," Perkins replied.

Antwan sat and listened to Ranson's direct order, while his thoughts and adrenaline began racing at the same time. The sun was beginning to rise, exposing the beautiful Yellow Stone mountain scenery. Yet, five hours into their manhunt, not a single word was spoken over their radios. That gave Antwan more of an advantage then anything because he knew these mountains and the rough terrain better than anyone.

Veronica had not told Antwan her entire story. In fact, the truth was that she was actually a mole sent to infiltrate the LAPD by none other than the Sinaloa Cartel. Her mission was to investigate and gather intel among the department about the senseless killings of hundreds of immigrants crossing the border, along with the massive increase of drugs and money taken from the Sinaloa Cartel.

After personally witnessing this horrific story, she couldn't hold back any longer. So, for the next two hours, she went into grave details, sharing secret information told to her by Antwan. Her uncle, Miguel, listened while taking it all in. He even asked Veronica to describe Antwan. He didn't want to get him confused with anyone else. He couldn't wait to retaliate. This was his golden opportunity to get his lick back. Miguel walked outside of his multi-million-dollar estate and instructed his army to get ready for war. They loaded up in over fifty SUVs and headed to Yellowstone National Park, which was two hours and fifteen minutes away...

As soon as the unit passed, Antwan emerged from behind a tree and joined them. Walking in sync, he then proceeded to tap the officer in front of him. He turned around only to a knife penetrating his throat. He was quietly laid down and covered with leaves as well. He kept a head count on the number of fatalities. The unit was headed in one big circle and they had no idea where they were. Knowing that, Antwan set a wire trip and climbed back up the tree to wait. He knew that it was just a matter of time before they returned, and the moment they did, he had something for them all.

Kelly was discovered by Perkins. His body was found slumped over in the driver's seat with his hands on the steering wheel, along with a note that read that Ranson and Perkins were next. Perkins screamed at the top of his lungs. He just couldn't believe his Unit had boots on the ground for more than twelve hours and still no Jacobs. *When you want something done you have to just do it yourself,* he thought to himself as he walked away.

Meanwhile, Antwan was observing from up in the tree as the Unit 12 group began to approach the wire trip he'd set.

The Cartel...

Miguel and his soldiers had finally arrived at Yellowstone National Park. As soon as they entered the property, he sent his unit in different directions. One by one, they exited their vehicles and swarmed the property like bees to honey. He'd already given them instructions along with a brief description of Antwan's height and features. It was war, and nobody else living was to be spared. Five minutes hadn't passed before Miguel began to hear excessive gunfire. He and several soldiers jumped into his vehicle and headed in that direction –

Booooom!!

The trip wire exploded upon impact. Antwan looked through his night vision binoculars and noticed right away that the Unit 12 tactical team was a hundred meters away, "Shit!" he said thinking that an animal may have walked onto it and tripped the wire. After the smoke finally cleared, he noticed an unidentified group of men standing around pointing their guns in different directions. He watched as they all began to retreat backward. Antwan knew by the way they were dressed, they weren't Yellow Stone Park Rangers or the Federal police.

He realized he had more company and didn't know how he was going to survive with this many ops raiding his father's estate. He knew his only option was to get back to his bunker where it was safe and just wait it out until Special Agent Hayes and the federal authorities arrived.

Down in the bunker...

Two hours passed and Antwan could still hear the explosions from the land mines and different wire trips exploding he'd set out. He grabbed his loaded AR-15 and pointed it straight up at the entrance of the manhole. He was willing to kill anyone or anything that opened the door. The chaotic massacre above his bunker between the cartel and Unit 12 sounded like Afghanistan!!!!

After an ongoing war for more than eight hours, seeing no signs of victory, Ranson was forced to make his men retreat, but not before giving out orders to blow up the estate.

Boom!!

The C-4 explosion shook the entire bunker. Everything that was hanging up was now just a big pile on the floor. ***Damn, what the hell could that have been?*** Antwan thought to himself. Three hours later, after the constant ringing in his ear finally went away, he could hear voices coming from above, but couldn't make out if it belonged to Hayes, or the opposition. All he knew was to listen out for the code word. Just when he was about to rest for the remainder of the night, he heard a loud voice over a bullhorn. It was saying Sunny Side Drive. Those words sounded to him as if Jesus was saying them himself. He was overwhelmed with joy knowing that he would be safe now.

Antwan proceeded to open the blast door with caution, slowly rising from the underground bunker only to realize that his father's entire estate was blown to ruins. At first glance, it resembled a scene out of a war movie – dead bodies, fires, Park rangers, FBI," and ambulances all decorated the chaotic five-acre property. Anthony Hayes stood in a grey suit, holding a bullhorn. Antwan walked over and shook his hand but was still in awe of his surroundings.

Back at internal affairs…

After five hours and fifteen minutes, Antwan was starting to feel as if he was under investigation. The vibe he was getting from investigator Hayes wasn't pleasant at all.

"I thought you and my father were partners at one time?" Antwan asked. "He spoke so highly of you and even told me that I could trust you. Should I be asking for a lawyer, because you've been making me feel as if I'm a suspect the entire time I've been sitting here. I want nothing more than to find the person responsible for my father's death and bring them to justice just as much as you.

Investigator Hayes paused for two minutes, he turned around and said, "So you are absolutely clueless to everything that's been going down, huh?"

"Antwan Jacobs, your father is not deceased! Our intelligence bureau states that he is currently alive and well. In fact, he has been under our radar for some time now." Investigator Hayes sat down directly in front of him and proceeded to open a thick file. "We believe that your father, Captain Dwayne Jacobs, has taken more than a hundred million in drugs and money and another fifty million in assault weapons from the Sinaloa Cartel and has been running an underground drug empire on the dark web for over two decades and the Sinaloa Cartel raged an ongoing war. He strategically placed you in the bunker on purpose for your protection, while he incited this ongoing war with the cartel. As long as he had you protected, nothing could stop him. This was a well-planned, thought-out, elaborate plot that he conspired all for his own personal gain and greed."

"But why would he send unit 12 to capture me then?" Antwan asked.

"After further investigation, we realized that it was all a smoke screen. Unit 12 had direct orders not to harm or to shoot at you at any time."

"Even after I've shot and killed several Unit 12 officers?"

"Unfortunately, they were casualties of war, but their names will not go down in vain. What your father placed down in the bunker with you were pennies, basically pardon gifts, and his personal smack in the face to the United States government. He needed to place you somewhere safe, so that he could continue his ongoing war with the Sinaloa Cartel."

"So, you telling me my dad faked his death and has been alive this entire time?"

"Correct, he was just recently spotted in Ontario Canada, and he is currently number five on our most wanted list. The United States government will not stop until he's in a jail cell alongside his archenemy, El Chapo. It's unfortunate you had to find out this way," investigator Hayes replied. "It's disappointing to me as well. Your father and I served side by side for over a decade. Him sitting in a jail cell is the last thing I could ever imagine."

"So, let's just say that everything we've discussed here is accurate, and you all supposed to have been investigating him the entire time. From my recollection, wasn't my father doing this as an active police officer?"

"Correct! He was under investigation because we didn't have any concrete evidence. Everything we had against him was circumstantial, but he decided to resign right before we indicted him. We believe he had a whistle-blower feeding him information from out of our federal district office."

"My father wasn't the person calling the shots, Brock Ranson was, and I know that for a fact!" Antwan said with confidence.

Investigator Hayes walked towards Antwan with another file in hand and proceeded to show him several aliases Dwayne was known to go under. It was there in the far right corner, in bold printed letters amongst other aka's.

Captain Dwayne Jacobs a.k.a. Brock Ranson

Antwan dropped his head to the table. This man, whom he looked up to as his superhero, was nothing more than a lying, evil, manipulating, money-hungry criminal.

"I'm at a lost for words Mr. Hayes."

"I understand, Antwan. We know that you had nothing to do with your father's actions. You've been granted full immunity and have received your orders to report back for duty at precinct 22 next week. I'll be sure to keep you updated if we come up with any new leads or to inform you of his arrest."

"Thank you," Antwan replied as he walked out of the federal internal affairs building in disbelief. So many thoughts and emotions were going through his mind. He just needed to rest up before he started his new position.

Three years later...

The California weather was perfect and Captain Antwan Jacobs was headed home from a long day of supervising his officers working the beat. He exited the Starbucks only to notice that a homeless man was standing next to his squad car. "Excuse me sir, can I help you?"

The homeless man never turned around, but his voice sounded so familiar that it gave him chills. "Don't look around or make any obvious moves. Stay calm, open the door, and sit me in the back of your squad car."

Immediately, Antwan did as he was told. He quickly entered his driver's seat and was told to continue looking forward.

"But Dad, what the hell – I miss you."

"I miss you as well, son."

"Dad, I know they have this story of you being a dirty cop all wrong. This has to be a mix-up."

"Unfortunately, son, they're as accurate as you're hearing it. I'm here today because I needed to personally apologize. You didn't deserve to have to go through any of this, but it was something I had to do or they were going to put me under the prison. So yes, I placed you in that bunker on purpose. I needed to know you were protected, so I built that bunker for that reason. I needed to have peace of mind while I continued my war against the government and cartel."

"But why, Dad!? You were one of the best – a top decorated detective for over twenty years –"

"Those accolades don't mean shit when you can't pay your mortgage on time. Scrambling to make ends meet and barely being able to put food on my table. I risked my life every single day for these people only to be given extra hours at Walmart. Eventually, I found my way. Even though it wasn't how I wanted this to end, I'm okay with it."

Antwan burst out in frustrating laughter, "Dad, you're sitting here telling me that you're okay with being one of the most wanted fugitives in the world?"

"Yes, and I'm ok with the choices I've made."

"So, what if I was to turn your ass in right now!? Antwan yelled at the top of his lungs.

"You would have every right to do so. Just know that it's always been bigger than me. They use cops as pawns also, son. The government and police officials are all corrupt. They just want me because I learned their game and mastered it."

"They estimated you stole over a hundred and fifty million in money, guns, and drugs. Is that true?" Antwan asked.

"It's true, but far from accurate. They dumbed it down for the tabloids. Son, I cracked the United States government and the Sinaloa Cartel heads for over a billion dollars in US currency alone. Collectively, they have been working together since the early nineties. It's sad to say, but it's literally no such thing as a war on drugs. Without drugs, this economy will crumble. It's a multi-trillion-dollar operation that I just happen to get a piece of, and they're mad."

"So, where do we go from here, Dad?"

"My hopes are that you would leave with me. I have an immaculate ten-bedroom estate in South Africa that I know you're going to love. You will never have to slave for these white people ever again. Just come with me, son."

Antwan began crying because he was conflicted. Although he loved his dad, he bled blue, and he made an oath to serve and protect regardless of the decisions his father made. He was different. Antwan started up the vehicle, stepped on the gas, and called into headquarters...

Five years later... in Johannesburg, South Africa

Dwayne walked out onto the deck of his four-hundred-and-fifty-foot luxury yacht. It was a pleasant day out, and he'd decided to sail to one of his exclusive estates in Cape Town. There, he would be conducting a conference amongst other millionaires and billionaires about the redevelopment of several subdivisions, schools, and projects within their communities.

It had been well over fifteen years since he went on the run from the United States government. He vowed to himself to never step another foot on American soil for as long as he lived. Even though several face reconstructions did him well, he just wasn't willing to take that risk. What he'd done for himself in

Africa was an amazing feat, to not only give back, but to give back to his beautiful black people just felt amazing. He made sure to give contributions as often as he could. In ten years, he'd donated well over twenty million dollars.

The meeting was held in his massive Great Room, and elites from all over Africa were all in attendance when the man of the hour walked in. "Good evening, ladies and gentlemen. Some of you, I know, and some I can't wait to meet. Welcome to the second annual Cape Town Conference of Black Wealth: Making A Difference. My name is Antwan Jacobs, and this beautiful woman beside me is my wife, Veronica Jacobs. We will be your host and hostess this evening."

Dwayne and Antwan Jacobs went on to live out the remainder of their lives serving and protecting the people they love. It was estimated in the African Forbes, with all of their business ventures and investments, that the Jacobs family's net worth, was over a quarter trillion dollars. For their generous contributions to their country, South African president, Cyril Ramaphosa, granted them both full immunity for as long as they were to never leave the country.

The United States government still has Dwayne, and Antwan Jacobs listed as two of the most wanted men in America.